Georgia Rises

A Day in the Life of Georgia O'Keeffe

Kathryn Lasky　　Pictures by Ora Eitan

MELANIE KROUPA BOOKS

FARRAR, STRAUS AND GIROUX • NEW YORK

The old lady's back feels crooked as a coiled rattlesnake. She has kinks in her calves, and her feet hurt. But still she wants to get up and get going. In twenty minutes the black of the night will fade away and that first lavender will begin to creep across the huge sky.

"Time to get up, Georgia!" she mutters.

She unrolls her night bun and combs out her nearly yard-long white hair. Then she twists it up again. She doesn't need a mirror to fix it right. She has been fixing this bun for more than fifty years. She takes off her nightgown and pulls on her long black dress and then her thick black stockings. She slips her feet into her soft cloth shoes.

She looks out the window again. The black is growing thin. The stars dim. "Hurry up, the lavender is coming," she whispers.

She makes hot water for her tea and pours cold water into the dogs' bowls. She sets her teacup down half-finished. And stretches her arms up high until she hears a tiny crack in her back. One crick gone, she thinks. Her feet don't feel too bad. She grabs her bag, her paint box and brushes, a canvas for painting, and her walking stick for scaring off rattlesnakes.

She walks through a narrow passageway and into a dirt courtyard, past the well in the middle. On the lid of the well, three black stones gleam in the grayness of the dawn. She stops to move one, then rearranges the two others. Now they look right. She walks through a door in the thick adobe wall into the desert.

As she stops and sniffs the spicy smell of the sagebrush, a raven flies overhead, printing its black wings against the gray sky. Georgia stretches again. Another crack, and another crick gone. She walks briskly, her eyes looking up.

The sky is purple now, and a slice of a silver moon still sails over the desert. She looks down at the path. A bone gleaming white sits as pretty as angel wings just ahead. Georgia likes bones. She picks up the bone and holds it high and closes one eye. The moon skims its top. She tilts the bone and captures the moon for one brief instant. The purple is already fading, draining out of the sky. The lavender will be here soon, she thinks.

She sets the bone on a rock and crouches low despite
a new pain in her back. If she sits down right on the desert
floor, she'll be comfortable. So she does, and takes out the
canvas and her paints.

"Aaah," she sighs. The sky is finally lavender, so pale it's
almost transparent, like the eyelids of babies. The shapes are
so simple—the wings of this bone reach up for the moon.

Georgia packs up the paints and brushes. She turns toward home. The lavender has faded from the sky. It is now the color of eggshells. The rust red hills are bleached by the rising sun. The black raven is back. It is becoming part of a painting in her imagination—the black V of the raven's wings held in the V of the rock hills. She'll keep the picture in her mind's eye.

Along the path on her way home, she picks up a rock and slips it into the deep pocket of her dress. Then she spots a chunk of wood no bigger than her fist that looks just like a ram's head. She picks it up, too.

Now Georgia walks back through the black door in the thick wall of the courtyard and into her house.

All day long Georgia will paint and think. She will think about bones and rocks, and the shape of the raven's wings as it floated over the hills.

She will climb a ladder to the roof of her house to watch the sky and hold a bone to the sun. It has a huge hole in the center, and she will watch the sky turn blue through that hole. How wonderful the white bone is against the blue. She has forgotten all about the lavender of the dawn and she is painting the blue of the afternoon. She has forgotten about the crick in her back and her sore feet. She is painting the whiteness of the bone.

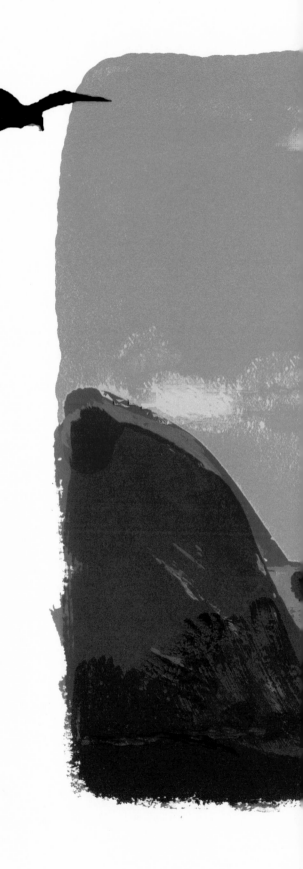

As the sun begins to slide down at the day's end, the hills that were bleached at noon turn red again. She picks up her stick and walks toward the sunset. Everything glows a deep pink-red. Even her own white hair in its neat little bun looks almost pink. She wants to paint those red hills, maybe this time not with the raven's wings but with a ram's head floating above them. She thinks of the chunk of wood she found at dawn. Her paintings grow shape by shape, bit by bit.

The sun slips away. Georgia stops. She loves the first few seconds after the sun is gone and the feel of the wind against her in this bare and open place.

It is twilight by the time she comes home. Just outside the walls of her house grows a beautiful flower. It blooms only in the evening and is very poisonous. It is called jimsonweed. She stops before she goes inside and looks into its white throat. She decides right then to paint that flower so big that people will have to look at it.

For dinner she eats a spicy stew of chicken with sweet chili peppers, beans, garlic, and onions. She drinks a cup of tea. The night is growing darker. The sky is clear. Soon the stars will climb into the huge blackness of the night and arrange themselves in figures. She must hurry, she must get to the night before the blackness comes.

She sets down her tea and goes outside to climb the ladder to the roof. Up she goes, climbing into the sky.

"Aaah," she sighs, for the sky is a deep blue and the slice of moon is so white in the sky tonight! How would the ladder she just climbed look floating against that mysterious blue sky between the hills now turned black and the white moon? It is a painting already in her head, ready to be put down tomorrow.

Georgia crawls down the ladder and goes in the house. She brushes her teeth and fixes her long white hair into a night bun. She pulls off her black stockings and her black dress. She puts on her nightgown and climbs into bed. Her back feels straight. She rubs her feet. They still hurt. But no matter. She will dream of green skies and white bones and the raven's wings. And tomorrow she will walk out into the desert to look for the lavender of the dawn sky.

Hurry up, Georgia—the lavender is coming!

Georgia O'Keeffe (1887–1986)

I was not a favorite child," Georgia O'Keeffe once said of her position in a family of five girls and two boys. She didn't mind, though; she felt it gave her more freedom. Growing up on a dairy farm in Sun Prairie, Wisconsin, Georgia had chores, but also time to play in the hayloft with her siblings or to spend alone, creating her own imaginary worlds. As the oldest girl, with an opinion on everything, she was the natural leader of her four sisters.

When Georgia was eleven, she took her first drawing class. By the time she was twelve, she announced, "I'm going to be an artist." Later, when she was graduating from high school, she was more determined than ever. "I am going to live a different life from the rest of you girls," she told her classmates. "I am going to give up everything for my art."

At seventeen, Georgia enrolled at the Art Institute of Chicago, but the following summer she came down with typhoid fever and had to drop out. Later, she studied at the Art Students League of New York, but financial difficulties made it impossible for her to continue. For several years she took various jobs, including teaching art, but she became discouraged with her own work. Georgia felt she was making drawings to please others, not herself.

Then, in Virginia, where her family now lived, she took a summer art class and was introduced to the ideas of Arthur Dow, who had been inspired by Japanese art. In 1914, when she was almost twenty-seven, Georgia moved back to New York to study with Dow. She began to experiment with abstract shapes and to reduce her use of color. "It's as if my mind can create shapes I don't even know about." Georgia had finally begun to make drawings to please herself.

In 1916, a friend showed Georgia's work to the well-known photographer Alfred Stieglitz, who exhibited her drawings in his New York gallery. That same year, she moved to the Texas panhandle to teach. She loved the Texas landscape, the blazing sunrises and glowing sunsets. "I found that I could say things with color and shapes that I couldn't say in any other way—things that I had no words for." A year later, when Georgia became seriously ill, Stieglitz sent a friend to bring her back to New York, where he could care for her. In 1924, the two married. They lived in New York City, spending summers at the Stieglitz home on Lake George in upstate New York, where Georgia painted in an old shed she called the Shanty. She rarely let anyone see her work—paintings of the lake, as well as close-up studies of flowers.

No artist ever painted a flower the way Georgia O'Keeffe painted flowers. She magnified the blossom until it covered a huge canvas, saying, "I'll paint it big and they will be surprised into taking time to look at it—I will make even busy New Yorkers take time to see what I see of flowers."

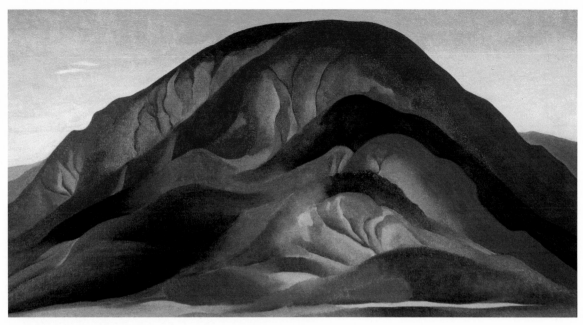

Rust Red Hills, 1930, by Georgia O'Keeffe (1887–1986). Oil on canvas, 16 x 30 inches, Sloan Fund Purchase, Brauer Museum of Art, 62.02, Valparaiso University, © 2005 The Georgia O'Keeffe Foundation / Artists Rights Society (ARS), New York.

In 1929, Georgia O'Keeffe found new inspiration in the landscape of New Mexico. Everything that she saw there, from the light to the clear colors and the mountains, impressed her. And perhaps because there were so few flowers in this high desert country, she began to paint bones. For Georgia, bones had nothing to do with death. "The bones," she said, "seem to cut sharply to the center of something that is keenly alive on the desert."

In New Mexico, she bought a house on eight acres of land called Ghost Ranch, and every summer for many years she would go there to paint. One summer she discovered an old adobe house with a large black door nearby. She was so taken by that door she became determined to buy that house, too. Some years later, in 1945, she did. She moved to this house in Abiquiu permanently in 1949, three years after Alfred Stieglitz died, and she would paint that black door many times.

With her walking stick in hand, Georgia continued to explore the hills outside her Abiquiu home, often in the company of her beloved chow dogs, Bo and Chia. In 1986, Georgia O'Keeffe died peacefully at the age of ninety-eight. She had become one of the most distinguished artists of her time. Her paintings can be found in museums and private collections across the country, including the Georgia O'Keeffe Museum in Santa Fe, New Mexico.

Author's Note

I have long admired Georgia O'Keeffe's life and paintings. Her independence of spirit and fierce dedication to her own inner vision helped me understand what it means to be an artist. My research for this book included several trips to New Mexico and a visit to her house in Abiquiu. I read and reread many of her letters to friends back East. These are full of details about her daily routine, her house, and even what she ate for breakfast and dinner. They also contain inspiring descriptions of the landscape near Abiquiu where she walked and painted almost every day. While my research has been extensive, *Georgia Rises* is historical fiction, an imaginative reconstruction of a day in O'Keeffe's life when she was in her seventies. In this picture book, O'Keeffe's ideas about several paintings, which she actually painted during different years, have been compressed into one day. My goal in *Georgia Rises* was to try to imagine what O'Keeffe saw and how she saw it—the light, the shadows, the color of the sky through the hole of a bone, and especially the excitement this woman felt getting up every morning to paint a world that she truly loved.

"Georgia O'Keeffe Painting in Her Car, Ghost Ranch, New Mexico, 1937." Photograph by Ansel Adams. Courtesy of Collection Center for Creative Photography, University of Arizona, © Trustees of the Ansel Adams Publishing Rights Trust.

Selected Bibliography

Georgia O'Keeffe. Produced and directed by Perry Miller Adato. Home Vision Entertainment. WNET/13, 1977.

Hassrick, Peter H., ed. *The Georgia O'Keeffe Museum*. New York: Harry N. Abrams (in association with the Georgia O'Keeffe Museum), 1997.

Lisle, Laurie. *Portrait of an Artist: A Biography of Georgia O'Keeffe*. New York: Washington Square Press / Simon & Schuster, 1997.

Loengard, John. *Georgia O'Keeffe at Ghost Ranch: A Photo-Essay*. New York: Stewart, Tabori and Chang, 1995.

Messinger, Lisa Mintz. *Georgia O'Keeffe*. London: Thames & Hudson, 2001.

O'Keeffe, Georgia. *Georgia O'Keeffe*. New York: Viking Press, 1976.

———. *Georgia O'Keeffe: Art and Letters*. Ed. Sarah Greenough. Essays by Jack Cowart and Juan Hamilton. Boston: New York Graphic Society Books / Little, Brown, 1987.

El Palacio: The Magazine of the Museum of New Mexico. "Special Issue: Georgia O'Keeffe." Vol. 102, No. 1 (1997).

Patten, Christine Taylor. Photographs by Myron Wood. *O'Keeffe at Abiquiu.* New York: Harry N. Abrams, 1995.

Robinson, Roxana. *Georgia O'Keeffe: A Life.* New York: Harper & Row, 1989.

Santa Fean. "Special Georgia O'Keeffe Collectors' Edition." Santa Fe, N.M. 1997.

Turner, Elizabeth. Essay by Marjorie P. Balge-Croz. *Georgia O'Keeffe: The Poetry of Things.* New Haven: Yale University Press, 1999.

Sources for quotes on pages 34–35

"I was not a favorite child"; "I'm going to be an artist"; and "I am going to live . . .": Robinson, *Georgia O'Keeffe: A Life,* pp. 18, 30, and 46.

"It's as if my mind . . .": Adato, *Georgia O'Keeffe* (a documentary).

"I found that I could say . . ." and "I'll paint it big . . .": O'Keeffe, *Georgia O'Keeffe,* pp. 13 and 23.

"The bones seem to cut . . .": Hassrick, *The Georgia O'Keeffe Museum,* p. 42.

In loving memory of my mother, Dvora
—Ora Eitan

Text copyright © 2009 by Kathryn Lasky
Pictures copyright © 2009 by Ora Eitan
All rights reserved
Distributed in Canada by Douglas & McIntyre Ltd.
Color separations by Embassy Graphics
Printed and bound in the United States of America by Worzalla
Designed by Robbin Gourley
First edition, 2009
1   3   5   7   9   10   8   6   4   2

www.fsgkidsbooks.com

Library of Congress Cataloging-in-Publication Data
Lasky, Kathryn.
    Georgia rises / by Kathryn Lasky ; pictures by Ora Eitan.
        p.   cm.
    Summary: The artist Georgia O'Keeffe spends the day transforming the materials, colors, and landscape of her desert home into paintings. Includes biographical notes.
        ISBN-13: 978-0-374-32529-9
        ISBN-10: 0-374-32529-4
    1. O'Keeffe, Georgia, 1887–1986—Juvenile fiction.   [1. O'Keeffe, Georgia, 1887–1986—Fiction.   2. Painting—Fiction.   3. Deserts—Fiction.   4. Artists—Fiction.]   I. Eitan, Ora, ill.   II. Title.

PZ7.L3274 Ge 2009
[E]—dc22

2004062603